P9-CBD-348

MID-YORK Library System
1600 Lincoln Avenue Utica, New York 13502

# COCK-A-DOODLE-DOO

words by Franz Brandenberg
pictures by ALIKI
Greenwillow Books, New York

For Adrian Želalić, and his mama and tata

The full-color art was created with black pen-and-ink line combined with watercolor paints, crayons, and colored pencils. The typeface is Spartan.

Text copyright © 1986 by Franz Brandenberg. Illustrations copyright © 1986 by Aliki Brandenberg. All rights reserved. No part of this book may be reproduced without permission in writing from Greenwillow Books, 105 Madison Avenue, New York, N.Y. 10016. Printed in Hong Kong by South China Printing Co.   First Edition   1 2 3 4 5 6 7 8 9 10

Library of Congress Cataloging in Publication Data:      Brandenberg, Franz.      Cock-a-doodle-doo.      Summary: The animal and human inhabitants of a farm quack, neigh, say, "Shoo! Shoo!" and otherwise communicate in their own fashion.   [1. Domestic animals—Fiction.   2. Farms—Fiction.   3. Animal sounds—Fiction]
I. Aliki, ill.   II. Title. PZ7.B3764Co 1986   [E]   85-9776   ISBN 0-688-06103-6   ISBN 0-688-06104-4 (lib. bdg.)

"Cock-a-doodle-doo!" said the cock.

The frog said, "Croak, croak."

The duck said, "Quack! Quack!"

The crow said, "Caw, caw."

The donkey said, "Ee-ah, ee-ah."

The dog said, "Woof! Woof!"

The sheep said, "Baa, baa."

The cow said, "Moo, moo."

# The farmer said, "Thank you!"

The horse said, "Neigh, neigh."

The turkey said, "Gobble, gobble."

The pig said, "Oink, oink."

The dove said, "Coo, coo."

The farmer's wife said, "Shoo! Shoo!"

"Cluck, cluck, cluck, cluck," said the hen.

The farmer's wife said, "Thank you!"

The baby said, "Mmmmm!"

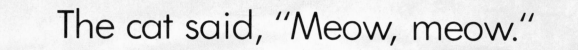

The cat said, "Meow, meow."

The mouse said, "Squeak! Squeak!"

"Buzz-z-z-z-z-z-z-z-z," said the bee.

The farmer's wife said, "Shoo! Shoo!"

# The cock said, "Cock-a-doodle-doo!"

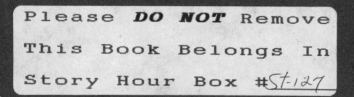

Please **DO NOT** Remove

This Book Belongs In

Story Hour Box #St-127